The Boxcar Children's Mysteries

The Boxcar Children
Surprise Island
The Yellow House Mystery
Mystery Ranch
Mike's Mystery
Blue Bay Mystery
The Woodshed Mystery
The Lighthouse Mystery
Mountain Top Mystery
Schoolhouse Mystery
Caboose Mystery
Houseboat Mystery
Snowbound Mystery
Tree House Mystery
Bicycle Mystery
Mystery in the Sand
Mystery Behind the Wall
Bus Station Mystery
Benny Uncovers a Mystery
The Haunted Cabin Mystery
The Deserted Library Mystery
The Animal Shelter Mystery
The Old Motel Mystery
The Mystery of the Hidden Painting
The Amusement Park Mystery
The Mystery of the Mixed-up Zoo
The Camp-out Mystery
The Mystery Girl
The Mystery Cruise
The Disappearing Friend Mystery
The Mystery of the Singing Ghost
Mystery in the Snow
The Pizza Mystery
The Mystery Horse
The Mystery at the Dog Show
The Castle Mystery
The Mystery of the Lost Village
The Mystery on the Ice
The Mystery of the Purple Pool
The Ghost Ship Mystery
The Canoe Trip Mystery
The Mystery of the Hidden Beach
The Mystery of the Missing Cat
The Mystery on Stage
The Dinosaur Mystery
The Mystery of the Stolen Music
The Chocolate Sundae Mystery
The Mystery of the Hot Air Balloon

Specials:

The Mystery in Washington, DC
The Mystery at Snowflake Inn
The Mystery at the Ballpark

THE MYSTERY OF THE HOT AIR BALLOON

created by
GERTRUDE CHANDLER WARNER

Illustrated by Charles Tang

SCHOLASTIC INC.
New York Toronto London Auckland Sydney

ISBN 0-590-20291-X

12 11 10 9 8 7 6 5 4 3 2 1 5 6 7 8 9/9 0/0

Printed in the U.S.A. 40

First Scholastic printing, July 1995

Contents

CHAPTER 1

Landing!

Benny sighed. "There's nothing to do," he said. Benny was six years old, and he liked to keep busy.

No one answered him. At the kitchen table, Violet was drawing, Jessie was reading a book on the history of flight, and Henry was looking through cookbooks.

"I wish we could go somewhere," Benny said. "Have an adventure."

The Aldens often took trips. They had adventures wherever they went.

"I can't go anywhere," Henry told him. "I'm too busy."

Mrs. McGregor, the Aldens' housekeeper, was away for the weekend. While she was gone, fourteen-year-old Henry was the cook.

"And I want to draw," Violet said. She was ten and a talented artist, but she never seemed to have enough time for her art-work.

"Reading this book is an adventure," twelve-year-old Jessie said. "It's all about flying."

Henry nodded. "I read that book," he said. "It was really interesting."

"Even if we weren't busy," Jessie said, "Grandfather said he wouldn't be home from the mill until late."

Benny had forgotten that. "Looks like everyone's busy but me," he said.

"Why don't you call some of your friends?" Violet suggested.

"Yes," Jessie agreed. "They could come here to play. I'll make popcorn."

"They're all busy, too," Benny told them.

Everyone was silent.

Finally, Violet said, "You could make another map."

Benny had made a map of the neighborhood. He liked drawing maps and he was good at it.

"No," Benny said. "I don't want to make a map today."

"Why don't you run your train?" Henry asked him.

Benny thought about that. He liked his electric train. When they first came to live with Grandfather Alden, he ran it every day. Lately, he'd been too busy with other things. "That's a good idea, Henry," Benny said.

Benny happily skipped out of the kitchen and went upstairs. He tiptoed down the long hall to his room. Outside the door, he paused to listen. Suddenly, he threw open the door. It was a game he played. He liked to pretend that the animals on his wallpaper — rabbits and dogs and bears — came to life when he left the room. He always hoped he would catch them at play. It never worked. The animals were always just as he had left them: wallpaper figures on a blue background.

"One of these days, I'll catch you," he told them.

He sat down on the floor beside his train engine. He turned it on, and the train began to move slowly along the track. He liked all the cars, but his favorite car was the boxcar. It looked just like the full-sized boxcar he and the other Aldens had lived in before coming to Grandfather's house, after their parents had died.

Benny quickly grew tired of the train. He turned it off and got on his rocking horse near the window. He liked to pretend it was a racehorse and he was a jockey. His feet touched the floor. He was growing too big for the rocking horse. A jockey could not be taller than his horse!

Benny walked to the window. From it he could see the whole yard. Near the fountain stood the old boxcar. Mr. Alden had had it moved here so the children could go out to see it anytime. They hadn't spent much time there lately. They were too busy.

"I haven't forgotten you, old boxcar," he said aloud.

Suddenly, a shadow fell across the lawn. An airplane, Benny thought. Too bad they couldn't go on a flight. That would be a good adventure.

Thc shadow couldn't belong to a plane; it was moving too slowly. And it was growing larger and larger!

Benny's mouth dropped open. Whatever was making the shadow was about to land on the lawn!

Benny raced out of his room and down the stairs.

"Something's landing on the lawn!" he shouted as he ran into the kitchen.

Watch, who had been sleeping at Jessie's feet, sat up and barked.

"Benny, don't be so noisy," Jessie scolded.

Henry looked up from his book. "Something's landing?" he said. "What? A pterodactyl?" he teased, but Benny didn't notice.

He ran to the window. "I don't know," Benny said. "Quick! Come look!"

Henry exchanged glances with Jessie and Violet. They all thought Benny was pretending he saw something to get their attention.

Just then, a shadow fell across the kitchen. The room grew dark. Watch's ears perked up. He whined and scooted under the table. The dog never acted like that without a reason.

Jessie pushed herself away from the table. "Maybe there *is* something out there," she said.

Violet put down her paintbrush.

Henry closed the cookbook and went to the door. He saw something hovering over the lawn. "It's an aerostat!" he said, his voice full of surprise and wonder.

"It looks like a big balloon to me," Benny said.

"An aerostat *is* a balloon," Henry told him, but Benny didn't hear him. He was already running outside.

Henry, Jessie, and Violet dashed after him.

A large basket hung below the balloon. Two people were inside it. Ropes hung from its sides.

"Grab those ropes!" Henry called.

Jessie reached out and took hold of a dangling rope. Violet and Jessie each grabbed other lines.

"Hold on tight!" Henry instructed.

The basket thumped to the ground and bounced.

Henry ran toward the collapsing balloon. He caught hold of a line at its crown.

The basket stopped moving and tipped over.

Afraid someone was hurt, Jessie gasped and put her hands over her eyes.

Laughing, a young man and woman in their late twenties crawled out.

"Are you all right?" Jessie asked.

"We're fine," the young woman assured Jessie. "Thanks to you."

Henry stepped forward. "Glad to help," he said. He extended his hand. "I'm Henry James Alden."

The woman smiled as she shook Henry's hand. "I'm Sky Blair." She turned to the young man at her side. "And this is Matt Farber."

"*Sky!*" Benny blurted out. "Your name is *Sky*?"

"Benny, remember your manners," Violet warned.

"Oh, it's all right," Sky said. "Everybody reacts like that." She smiled at Benny. "My parents wanted an unusual name. They didn't know I'd end up as a balloon pilot."

Henry introduced his sisters and brother. "We're happy to meet you," he said.

Matt laughed. "I'll bet you've never met anyone who landed on your lawn before."

"Never!" the Aldens all said at once.

"We didn't intend to land here," Sky said. "A sudden gust of wind blew us off course."

"Don't you have a steering wheel or something?" Benny asked.

Sky rolled her blue eyes. "Don't I wish," she answered.

"An aerostat is pretty much at the mercy of the breezes," Jessie said.

"You seem to know a lot about ballooning," Matt said.

"I'm reading a book on the history of flight," Jessie explained. "I just finished the section on hot air balloons, and now a balloon lands on the lawn!"

"Where'd you come from?" Benny asked Sky.

"Lloyd's Landing," she told him.

The Aldens knew about that town. They often drove through it.

"That's a long way away," Benny said.

"Not in a balloon." Sky pointed upward. "There're no stoplights or traffic up there."

"How will you get back?" Violet asked.

"That's a problem," Matt answered. "We lost contact with our chase crew."

"Chase crew?" Benny repeated.

"Every flight is followed by a ground crew," Sky explained. "They meet us at the landing site."

"We use two-way radios to keep in touch," Matt said. "Something happened to ours. I think the batteries gave out."

Sky narrowed her blue eyes. "That shouldn't have happened," she said.

Matt held up his hands. "I know. I should've checked."

"Could you phone someone?" Henry asked.

"We could, yes," Sky said. "Would you mind if we used your phone? We'll call the balloon port. The chase crew probably returned there when we lost contact."

"What's a balloon port?" Benny asked.

"It is usually near an open field," Sky answered. "It's where we launch the balloon."

Henry invited them inside.

"Would you like a cold drink?" Jessie asked.

"We sure would," Matt said.

While they waited for the chase crew, Matt and Sky drank lemonade and talked about ballooning.

"We're going to start a ballooning business in Lloyd's Landing. We'll take people up for rides and also teach them how to balloon," Sky told them. "It's the perfect place to do this."

"And we're holding a rally this weekend to advertise the opening," Matt added.

"Will there be lots of people there?" Benny asked. He imagined the sky full of colorful balloons. What a sight that must be!

Matt laughed. "We hope so."

"How would you like to come to the rally?" Sky asked. "We could use your help."

"You're a good crew," Matt agreed. "And when the rally's over, we'll take you up in the balloon."

Benny's eyes grew big. This was the adventure he had hoped for. "We'll be there!"

"Wait a minute, Benny," Jessie said. "We have to ask Grandfather first."

The doorbell rang. They all went to answer. Henry opened the door. A tall, thin man stood outside.

Sky said, "Are we glad to see you!" She introduced him to the Aldens. His name was Pete Moran, and he owned an old inn in Lloyd's Landing. "He's a volunteer crew member."

"Won't you come in?" Jessie asked politely.

"I could use something cold to drink," Pete answered. "Chasing balloons is hard work."

Jessie poured him a glass of lemonade.

"Alden?" he said as he set the glass on the tray. "Do you have a relative named *James Henry Alden*?"

"That's our grandfather," Henry answered. "I have the same names, only reversed."

Pete shook his head. "It certainly is a small

world." He went on to explain that his father and Mr. Alden had been friends. "I haven't seen your grandfather in years."

"Maybe you'll have the chance to see him this weekend," Sky told him. "I've invited the Aldens to the rally."

"That'd be great," Pete said.

"We're not sure we can come," Jessie said.

"Grandfather is very busy," Violet added.

Henry said, "With all the people coming to the rally, there's probably nowhere to stay."

"There's always room for an Alden at The Landing's Inn," Pete said.

Benny grinned. "Grandfather'll let us go. He just has to!"

CHAPTER 2

Grandfather's News

Once the basket and balloon were secured in a small trailer, Sky said to the Aldens, "Let's hope we'll meet again soon." Then she got into Pete Moran's station wagon. *The Landing's Inn* was written on its side. As it pulled out of the driveway, Pete, Sky, and Matt waved. The Aldens waved back. Then they went inside.

"Let's call Grandfather," Benny suggested. He was bursting to tell him all about the balloon rally.

"No, Benny," Jessie said. "We'll just have to wait to tell him about the rally until he comes home."

Benny groaned. Waiting always seemed to take longer than anything else.

"Look here," Henry said. He picked up a newspaper from a chair. It was called *The Landing Times.* "Pete must have left it."

"Does it say anything about the rally?" Violet asked.

Henry turned a page. "Here's an ad for the inn." He read, " 'The Landing's Inn: Best Bed and Breakfast in the County.' "

"Breakfast?" Benny asked. "What about lunch and dinner?"

Jessie laughed. "I'm sure they wouldn't let you starve, Benny."

"Oh, here's something about the rally," Henry said. "It's an editorial." He read the article to himself.

"What does it say?" Violet asked.

"Mostly, it asks questions," Henry answered. " 'Does Lloyd's Landing want this new business?' " he quoted. " 'What will ballooning do to this peaceful community? Is it safe?' It goes on like that."

"Does it give any answers?" Jessie wanted to know.

"No answers," Henry responded. "It just says the townspeople should consider these questions."

"Why wouldn't the town want ballooning?" Benny wondered aloud. "It looks like so much fun."

"Is it safe?" Violet asked.

"If you'rc trained properly, it's safe," Jessie said.

"What could *ballooning* do to Lloyd's Landing?" Benny asked.

"It could bring lots of people to town," Violet suggested.

"That could be good for the other businesses," Jessie said.

Benny nodded. "People have to eat," he said. "That could be good for the restaurants."

"And they have to sleep," Henry said.

"So that could be good for the motels and inns," Violet concluded.

The Aldens couldn't think of a single reason why anyone would object to a hot air balloon business in their town.

"I suppose some people just don't like new things," Henry said.

The door flew open and Grandfather rushed in. "I have good news!" he announced.

Benny jumped up. "So do we!"

Violet poked him. "Grandfather first," she said.

Grandfather pulled out a chair and sat down. "Do you remember Lloyd's Landing?" he asked.

The children looked at each other. Could Grandfather's news have something to do with the balloon rally? Barely able to contain their excitement, they all said, "Yes!"

"I've just learned there will be a hot air balloon rally there this weekend," Mr. Alden continued. "I left work early to tell you about it."

The younger Aldens began to laugh.

Grandfather looked puzzled. "What's so funny?" he asked.

"We know all about the rally," Benny answered.

Henry told him about the hot air balloon landing in the yard.

Grandfather laughed. "I can never surprise you!" he said. "You're just too smart for me!" Then his tone grew serious. "I don't suppose you want to go to the rally. You're all so busy." But his eyes were twinkling.

"We want to go!" Benny exclaimed. "We want to go!"

"There is one problem," Mr. Alden said. "I'm not sure there'll be a place to stay and driving back and forth every day would not be practical."

Jessie told him about Pete Moran and his invitation to stay at The Landing's Inn for the weekend.

"That settles it. It will be so good to see Pete after all these years," Grandfather said.

"May Soo Lee come with us?" Violet asked.

Seven-year-old Soo Lee was the Aldens' cousin. She had been adopted by Cousins Joe and Alice.

"Of course," Mr. Alden said. "And we'll ask Joe and Alice to take care of Watch." He went to the phone. "I'll call the inn to tell them we'll be there bright and early tomorrow morning."

"You see?" Benny said. "I knew Grandfather would let us go."

Late the next morning, Mr. Alden swung the station wagon into The Landing's Inn brick driveway. "You go on ahead," he told the others. "Henry and I will bring in the luggage."

Benny hopped out of the car. Soo Lee, Violet, and Jessie followed. They paraded up the wide stairs and across the open porch to carved wood double doors. One of them was ajar.

"Should we knock?" Benny asked.

"I think we just go in," Jessie answered. She pushed open the door and stepped aside to let the others enter.

No one was in the large entry hall.

"What do we do now?" Benny whispered.

"Shhh," Jessie said. She pointed toward a set of closed doors across the hall. Behind them, the sound of voices rose and fell. Someone was arguing.

"Mary, you're wrong!" one voice said. "I've made up my mind."

Another voice said, "I'll never understand you, Barbara!"

"Sometimes we just have to do what we have to do," the first voice said.

Then Grandfather and Henry came in.

"Anyone here?" Mr. Alden called.

The voices hushed. Then, silence. Suddenly the doors to the closed room slid open, and an older woman came out, rushed down the hall and out the side door.

She had stopped for a moment to adjust her clothes. Her hair, her clothes — everything about her was neat and clean.

Shortly after, another woman came out to greet them.

Grandfather Alden giant-stepped across the room. "Barbara!" he said and gave her a big hug. "It is so nice to see you!"

The woman smiled, but her eyes were sad. "It's good to see you, too," she said.

Mr. Alden introduced the children. "This is Barbara Moran, Pete's wife," he said. "She and Pete own the inn."

"Welcome," Barbara said. "Your rooms are ready." She did not look at them. Instead, she stared out the window and watched the woman with the perfect hair get into her car.

"Is there something wrong, Barbara?" Mr. Alden asked. "Where's Pete?"

Barbara's face reddened. "Oh, no, nothing," she answered. "I'm just a little upset about something. Pete will be back soon. He just ran out to take care of an errand. I thought he'd be back before you arrived." She smiled. "Let me show you your rooms."

She led them up the curved staircase and down a narrow hall. "I've given you adjoining rooms and bath," she said and opened two doors.

Henry, Benny, and Mr. Alden went into one room; Jessie, Violet, and Soo Lee into the other. The rooms were large with high ceilings and tall, narrow windows. They were furnished with antiques. Between the two rooms was a big bathroom.

Barbara said, "If there's anything you need, just ask."

"It looks as if you've thought of everything," Mr. Alden responded.

"When you're settled, come downstairs. I'll make tea," Barbara said.

"I hope there's going to be something else besides tea," Benny said when Barbara left. "I'm — "

" — hungry," the others chimed in.

Mr. Alden was the first one ready. "I'll meet you downstairs," he told Soo Lee and his grandchildren. "I'd like to visit with Barbara."

After he had gone, Henry said, "Barbara seemed . . . strange."

"Because of the argument," Violet said.

Henry looked puzzled. "What argument?"

"We heard her arguing with another woman," Soo Lee explained.

"Before you and Grandfather came in," Jessie added.

"The other woman — her name was *Mary*," Benny put in. "I saw her leave. She was all dressed up."

"I wonder what they were arguing about?" Jessie said.

"Probably nothing to do with us," Henry said.

CHAPTER 3

Too Many Questions

When the Aldens came downstairs, Barbara met them in the entry hall. "Come into the parlor," she said and led them into the room where the argument had taken place.

Grandfather was already there.

A table in the center of the room was set with juice, tea, coffee, and plates of pastries and breads.

"Oh, boy," Benny said. "Does it smell good!"

"It tastes good, too," Grandfather assured him.

"Help yourselves," Barbara told them.

They filled their plates and sat down.

"Have you lived here long, Mrs. Moran?" Jessie asked politely.

Barbara laughed. "Oh, my, yes," she said. "All my life. I love this old town. Please call me Barbara." She seemed to relax for the first time since the Aldens' arrival.

"Barbara's grandparents and the Lloyds founded Lloyd's Landing," Grandfather explained. "Does Mary still live here?" he asked Barbara.

"Mary?" she repeated as though she'd never heard the name before. "Ah, yes, she's — uh — still . . . here."

Mary. That was the name of the woman Barbara had been arguing with. Benny poked Violet. She gave him a warning glance.

"Mary who?" Benny asked.

"Mary England," Grandfather answered. "She's the Lloyds' granddaughter. As I remember she left town — wanted to see the world — but it wasn't long before she realized there was no place like home."

"That's for sure," Benny said. He took his plate back to the table for seconds.

Sky and Matt came in.

Sky looked surprised and happy. "You made it!" she said.

Benny's smile was wide. "I told you we would."

Grandfather stepped forward and introduced himself.

"You must be the grandfather we've heard so much about," Matt said as he shook Mr. Alden's hand.

"And you two must be the adventurers *I've* been hearing so much about," Grandfather responded. "Are you staying here, too?"

"For the time being," Matt answered. "We rented a store in town. There's an apartment above it. We have some work to do on it before we can move in."

"As soon as everything's ready," Sky added, "we're getting married."

Everyone except Barbara said, "Congratulations."

Soo Lee was thinking about their store. She pictured it in the center of town. Surely, they couldn't launch balloons from there. "Where do you . . . take off?" she asked.

Sky seemed to know what she was thinking. She laughed. "We'd certainly stop traffic if we tried to launch a balloon in the middle of Main Street."

"The balloon port is just outside town," Matt explained. "The store is our headquarters."

"No matter where you launch them," Barbara said, "balloons will stop traffic."

"That could be good for this old town," Mr. Alden said. "Put some life into it."

Barbara shot him a disbelieving glance. "There's nothing wrong with this town," she said. After a pause, she laughed nervously. "Oh, dear. I didn't mean to snap at you. It's just that I don't understand why Sky and Matt chose Lloyd's Landing for their business."

Matt smiled. "For the reason you said: There's nothing wrong with this town."

"It's a very charming town," Sky put in. "We looked all over before deciding to open our business here."

"Yes, but with all the hills and the forests, won't it be dangerous?" Barbara asked.

"Ballooning is dangerous only when the pilot is untrained or takes risks," Matt answered.

"Balloonists enjoy beautiful scenery," Sky said. "Lloyd's Landing has plenty of that."

"We're so far from the main highway," Barbara said. "Wouldn't it be more profitable to locate closer to . . . traffic?"

Sky laughed. "If we wanted to make lots of money," she responded, "we wouldn't be in the ballooning business."

Barbara kept asking questions.

Finally, Henry said, "I read a newspaper article about this — are the townspeople against the business coming to town?"

Barbara's face reddened. She picked up the

coffeepot. "Excuse me," she said. "I'll get more coffee." She hurried away.

"Have you been having trouble with the local people?" Mr. Alden asked Matt.

"No trouble, really," Matt answered. "They don't know anything about ballooning so it makes them a little . . . edgy."

"We bought the property," Sky said. "It's ours. We have every right to be here."

Barbara came in from the kitchen. "Mr. Alden, there's a telephone call for you. You can take it in the hall."

Grandfather sighed. "I hope it's not the mill."

But it was. "I'm sorry, but I have to get back home," he said when he returned. "I'm needed at the mill."

The children tried to hide their disappointment, but it was difficult.

"Don't look so sad," Mr. Alden told them. "I think we can work this out."

Barbara said, "The children are welcome to stay here. I'll keep an eye on them."

"They're very independent," Grandfather

said. "I'm sure they won't be any trouble."

"I'll be happy to have them," Barbara said.

"They'll be out at the port with us most of the time," Sky put in. "We're on our way out there now. Would you like to ride along?" she asked the children.

Suddenly, Benny was no longer hungry. He set his plate on the table. "Would we ever!"

"Good. Then it's settled," Mr. Alden said. He hugged each of his grandchildren. "I'll pick you up on Sunday evening."

"Is everybody ready?" Sky asked.

They were.

"Well then, let's go!" She headed for the door.

The children followed.

"Oh, Benny," Grandfather said. "Aren't you forgetting something?"

Benny cocked his head. "Am I?" he said.

"Your second helping of this delicious cinnamon bread."

"Oh, that's all right," Benny said. "I've had enough."

CHAPTER 4

The Runaway Balloon

"Look!" Soo Lee shouted. Sitting in the back of Sky's van, she pointed out the window.

"It's a balloon!" Benny exclaimed.

To their right, a brightly colored balloon drifted high above the trees.

"*Who* could that be?" Matt wondered.

Behind the wheel, Sky was not so calm. "Whoever it is is in big trouble," she said. "No one's supposed to go up until we're there."

"It seems to be coming down," Violet observed.

"It just looks that way," Henry said.

Matt thrust his head out the window. "No, no. Violet's right! The balloon *is* coming down!"

"It can't be," Sky said. "It's over the woods. If it comes down there, it'll get tangled in the trees."

Trying to keep the balloon in sight, they drove along the road. Coming to a large, open field filled with trucks and people preparing their balloons for flight, Sky turned in and stopped. She hopped out of the van and ran toward a small group of people, shouting, "Who's up there?"

Matt and the Aldens raced after her.

A large man broke from the group. "If this is the way you're going to run things, you'll never be successful," he said.

"Who's up there?" Sky persisted.

"Who knows," the man answered. "Your whole operation is a disaster."

He kept talking, but Sky wasn't listening.

She turned to the others gathered there. "Did anyone see who launched that balloon?" she asked.

No one had.

"Don Fister was the only one here when we arrived," a woman said.

Don Fister, the man who was complaining, snapped, "Oh, no! You're not going to blame me for this. That balloon was airborne when I got here."

"Calm down, Don," Sky said. "No one's blaming you for anything."

Another woman hurried over to the scene. Although the woman's graying hair was windblown, and she wasn't wearing white gloves, Benny recognized her. He poked Jessie. "That's the woman we saw leave the inn," Benny whispered.

"What woman?" Jessie asked.

"You know — Mary. The one who was arguing with Barbara."

"I was afraid of something like this," Mary was saying. "Too many trees for ballooning. It's just not safe. You should rethink this,

Ms. Blair. There are plenty of places more suitable for your business."

"Business? Ha!" Don Fister said. "It's a joke, that's what it is. They don't have a business. They have a plan for failure."

Sky wasn't paying any attention. "Come on, Matt," she said. "We have to go after that balloon." She turned and headed toward the van.

The Aldens hung back. Should they go along? Would they bc in the way?

Matt answered their unspoken question. "Hurry!" he said to them. "That balloon's in trouble! We can't waste a minute!"

"That Don Fister sure was nasty," Benny commented as they drove away from the launch site.

Matt waved his hand. "Don't pay any attention to him," he said. "He's full of hot air."

"Like the balloons," Soo Lee said.

Benny laughed. "That's a good joke, Soo Lee."

Sky laughed, too. "And true," she said.

"Don owns a balloon business a few hours away. He thinks he's the only one who knows anything about ballooning. But I must admit, he's a crackerjack balloonist."

"Yeah," Matt agreed. "He doesn't like us but he never misses a rally. Don loves competition."

They made several wrong turns before they found the balloon. It was suspended from an oak tree at the edge of a small clearing in the forest preserve.

"The basket looks empty," Jessie said as they climbed out of the van.

"Let's hope it is," Sky said.

Matt climbed the tree. Looking down into the basket, he said, "It's empty all right."

"How's the balloon?" Sky asked.

Matt examined the brightly colored cloth. "Looks pretty good. No big tears. Now, if I can just — "

They all held their breath as Matt reached out to release the balloon.

"Got it!"

The basket fell at their feet with a thud.

The deflated balloon floated down on top of it.

"This balloon is small," Benny observed.

Struggling to help fold it, Henry said, "It looks big to me."

"Me, too," Soo Lee put in.

"Compared to ours, this balloon *is* small," Matt said.

"Ours can carry a larger basket — which means more people can fit inside," Sky added.

Everyone helped pack the balloon and basket into the van.

On the way back to the port, Henry asked, "How did the balloon escape?"

"Someone had to inflate it and let it go," Matt explained.

"Maybe it was an accident," Violet suggested.

"Right," Benny said. "Probably whoever blew it up, didn't mean to let it go."

"Possible," Sky said, "but not likely."

"Wouldn't the owner of the balloon have said something?" Jessie asked.

"I should think so," Sky said. "The owner would be very upset."

Suddenly Soo Lee said, "Maybe someone *meant* to let the balloon go."

Matt nodded. "I think you're right, Soo Lee. This was no accident."

Before the van had come to a complete stop, a man ran up waving his arms and shouting.

"I think I know who owns the runaway balloon," Matt said.

"Brad Golder," Sky said.

At the van window, Brad Golder, a thin, balding man, asked urgently, "Did you find it? Did you find my balloon?"

Sky pointed her thumb toward the back of the van. "Relax, Brad. Everything's under control," she assured him.

"Under control? Is that what you think? Someone steals my balloon and you say everything's under control?"

Matt came around the side of the van and put his hand on Brad's shoulder.

"What happened, Brad?" Matt asked.

"Where were you when your balloon was launched?"

Trying to calm himself, Brad took several deep breaths. Then he said, "I left my gear near my truck and went into town for breakfast. When I got back here, it was gone. Don told me my balloon was in the sky. I've been frantic." He began to pace. "If anything's happened to that balloon, you're responsible. If this is the kind of business you're going to run, maybe we don't need it around here."

"It looks all right," Sky told him. "Why don't we get it out and take a look."

Sky opened the back of the van, and they hoisted the balloon down.

As they spread out the balloon, Don Fister wandered over. "That balloon's a goner," he said. "This whole operation is over before it starts."

"Listen, Fister," Matt said. "You're wrong."

"Let's take a look at this," Sky said changing the subject as she began to examine the balloon spread out before them.

They went over the nylon covering inch by inch. Brad found a small tear. "Easy to repair," he decided. He was obviously relieved that there was so little damage.

Mary joined the group. Benny noticed that her hair was still messy.

"Is everything under control here?" she asked.

Henry spoke up. "Yes, ma'am," he said. "Mr. Golder's balloon wasn't badly damaged."

"Ah, but it *could* have been. That is the point," she said. Without smiling she thrust out her hand. "I'm Mary England. I don't believe we've met. Pleased to meet you, I'm sure," she said.

The Aldens didn't think she seemed at all pleased.

At the other side of the field, a car pulled in. A man got out.

"There's the press," Don Fister commented. "Wait until they find out about this little misadventure."

CHAPTER 5

More Trouble

An older man approached. His glasses were perched on the top of his head. Under his arm was a large brown envelope.

"Is he a reporter?" Jessie asked.

"That's Hollis McKnight," Sky answered. "He's the owner and editor of *The Landing Times*, the local newspaper." She started toward him. "Oh, Mr. McKnight, I have the money for the ad," she told him.

Mr. McKnight said, "I'll get the money later. Right now I have to speak with Mary."

He took Mary England's arm and led her away.

"Did you tell McKnight what's been going on around here?" Don Fister said.

Matt ignored him.

Sky touched Matt's arm. "Come on, Matt," she said. "Don will cool off. In the meantime, let's show the Aldens what this balloon business is all about." She started toward a small shed at one corner of the field.

The Aldens followed.

"One of these days, we're going to enlarge this storage shed," Sky told them.

"We're going to make it into a lounge," Matt added. "With tables and chairs."

"And a big window so people can see the balloons ascend," Sky said.

"Will there be anything to eat?" Benny asked.

"A well-equipped snack bar," Matt answered.

Benny was glad to hear that.

At the shed, Sky said, "Tomorrow you'll be part of our chase crew."

"And you'll help with the launch," Matt added.

"Wait here," Sky instructed. "We want to show you some of our equipment." She and Matt unlocked the shed and went inside.

Not far away, Hollis McKnight and Mary England were in a heated conversation.

"What do you suppose that's all about?" Henry wondered aloud.

"Why is Mary's hair all messed up?" Benny asked. "She looks like she'd always be combed. Not like me."

"Probably the wind," Violet suggested.

Soo Lee looked around. She studied a nearby tree. Not a single leaf was moving. "There is no wind," she said.

"She probably had her car windows open," Jessie decided.

"What's Mr. McKnight doing?" Henry said.

The man pulled a stack of something — letters? — from the brown envelope. He waved them in Mary's face. She turned away.

Mr. McKnight kept talking. Suddenly, Mary turned around to face him. She said something and dug in her purse. Whatever she pulled out flashed in the sunlight.

"It's a mirror," Henry said.

"And a comb," Violet added as Mary began smoothing her hair.

Sky came out of the shed. Matt followed, carrying a metal box.

"This is the instrument package," Sky told the Aldens.

They crowded around as Matt lifted the flight instruments out of the box.

Sky pointed to a round dial. "This is the variometer," she said. "It tells us our vertical speed."

Matt pointed to another gauge. "Altimeter," he identified. "It tells us our altitude — how high up in the sky we are. And that last dial measures the temperature inside the balloon."

"Why do you have to know the temperature inside the balloon?" Soo Lee asked.

"The air in the balloon has to be kept at

just the right temperature or the balloon will not do what the pilot wants it to," Matt answered.

"How do you heat the air?" Violet asked.

"Propane gas," Sky answered. "You'll see the tanks later."

Benny studied the instruments. Even Grandfather's station wagon had more dials. "Are these all the instruments you need?"

"A compass helps," Sky said.

"And a map," Matt added.

"I'm good at map reading," Benny said proudly. "I even made a map of our neighborhood."

Sky smiled. "Good. Tomorrow, when you're part of the chase crew, those skills will come in handy."

Hollis McKnight joined the group. "I'll take that money now, Ms. Blair," he said.

Sky dug her wallet from her back pocket. "I've made a couple of changes in the ad copy," she said. She handed Mr. McKnight a check and a folded piece of paper. "Do you want to go over them?"

Mr. McKnight shook his head. "I'm sure I'll be able to figure out the changes." Then he walked away.

Don Fister ran up beside him. "Mr. McKnight," he said, "let me tell you what's been going on here."

McKnight waved him away, saying, "Not now. Not now."

"What kind of newspaper editor are you?!" Don Fister shouted after him. Then, he stomped off.

Matt shook his head. "That Don is nothing but trouble," he said.

Sky didn't respond. Instead, she went on talking about ballooning. "Teamwork is the most important aspect of ballooning," she said. "Everyone has a job. And they must do it well."

The Aldens became so interested in their ballooning lessons they didn't hear Pete Moran pull in.

"Lunch!" Pete announced as he opened the back of the station wagon.

Benny heard that. So did everyone else.

Balloonists quickly gathered near the station wagon. Using the back of the station wagon as a table, Pete spread out an assortment of cold salads and breads.

Henry stepped forward. "Do you need help?" he asked Pete.

Pete nodded. "You could hand out the plates."

Henry took the paper plates and stood beside the station wagon. Jessie took the plastic utensils.

A line formed. The first person was about to eat when Brad Golder shouted at Pete, "You're the one who launched my balloon!"

CHAPTER 6

A Suspect

Pointing at Pete Moran, Brad Golder said, "You!"

Pete's mouth dropped open. "I — I — don't know what you're talking about," he sputtered.

Matt stepped forward. "Wait a minute, Brad," he said. "What makes you think Pete launched your balloon?"

Brad pointed his finger. "His back pocket," he answered.

Looking puzzled, Pete reached behind him

and pulled a red-and-white bandanna from his pocket.

"That's my bandanna!" Brad said.

Sky took the scarf from Pete. "It's just a red bandanna," she said. "It could be anybody's."

"Look in the corner," Brad directed. "You'll see my initials."

Sky did as he directed. Sure enough, the letters *B. G.* were written in black ink.

"I always tie two bandannas to my balloon basket: a red one and a blue one. For luck," Brad explained.

"I didn't launch your balloon," Pete told him. "I found that bandanna this morning on my way back from the farmers' market. I was buying fruit and vegtables for the inn. I stopped at the spring on Mill Road for a cool drink. The bandanna was lying on the ground."

"That's true," Mary England said. "I saw Pete on Mill Road early this morning."

After that, no one said anything for what

seemed like a long time. Finally, Brad mumbled something and walked off.

Pete looked after him. Then, he turned to the waiting group. He forced a smile and said, "Let's eat."

"Good idea," Benny said.

The Aldens took their plates to a tree at the edge of the field.

"If I'd known we would have a picnic, I would have brought our blue cloth," Jessie said. The blue tablecloth was a reminder of their days in the boxcar.

"And I would have brought my old pink cup," Benny put in.

"We'll do fine without those things," Henry said.

They sat in a circle in the shade of the oak.

Mopping his forehead with a large white handkerchief, Hollis McKnight came up to them. "More trouble?" he asked as he adjusted his glasses.

"No, sir," Henry answered.

"Then what was all that commotion by Pete's station wagon?"

Henry nodded. "Oh, that," he said. "Brad Golder thought Pete Moran launched his balloon."

"Now why would he think that?" Mr. McKnight asked.

Jessie told him about the bandanna.

"Pete's telling the truth," he said. "I saw him out by the spring this morning."

"Mary England saw him, too," Benny told him.

Mr. McKnight glanced down at Benny. His eyes looked very big behind his glasses. "Mary? She told you that? Well, that proves Pete wasn't anywhere near the port." Then he said, "Enjoy your lunch," and hurried away.

"That was strange," Violet said.

"I thought so, too," Jessie agreed.

"Why?" Benny asked.

"I don't think he came over to see what was going on between Brad and Pete," Jessie explained.

"Instead, he waited to ask us about it," Violet added.

"A good newspaper person likes to get the information firsthand," Henry said.

"Maybe he's not a good newspaper person," Benny said.

"He seemed to know all about the runaway balloon," Soo Lee commented.

"Everybody knows about that," Benny said.

Henry understood what Soo Lee meant. "That's right," he said. "Don Fister tried to tell him about it, but Mr. McKnight wouldn't listen."

"Someone else probably told him," Jessie said.

"Mary might have told him," Violet suggested.

They ate silently, thinking about this morning's events.

"Do you think Pete launched the balloon?" Benny asked after a while.

"Oh, I don't think he would do such a thing," Jessie answered.

"He couldn't have done it alone," Henry said.

Remembering this morning's argument at the inn, Violet said, " 'Sometimes we just have to do what we have to do.' "

"What does that mean?" Henry asked.

"It's what Barbara said to Mary this morning at the inn," Jessie answered. "When they were arguing."

"Maybe Barbara and Pete launched the balloon," Benny said.

"Barbara was at the inn with us this morning," Soo Lee reminded them.

"But Pete wasn't," Benny said. "Barbara told us he was running errands."

"He just told us he was at the farmers' market," Jessie said.

"He could have been fibbing," Soo Lee said.

"Right," Benny agreed. "Maybe Barbara was nervous because she knew he was launching the balloon, and she was afraid he'd get caught."

Violet shook her head. "Pete didn't do it," she said firmly. "He's too nice."

"And why would he?" Benny said.

CHAPTER 7

Hare and Hounds

"Time for our first competition!" Sky announced suddenly.

"We're starting with *Hare and Hounds.*" She explained that one balloon, the hare, would take off first. Shortly after, the other balloons would follow. Whoever landed closest to the hare would win.

"Who's the hare?" someone asked.

"We'll choose by lottery," Matt said. He held up a bowl. In it were folded slips of paper. "On one of these is the word *hare.*"

Excitement shot through the group as the pilots lined up. One by one, they reached into the bowl. One after another, they said, "Hound."

Don Fister pulled out his paper. He read it, then held it high over his head. "Hare!" he proclaimed.

Sky handed each pilot a map.

Matt said, "I just talked with the weather service. Conditions are perfect." He turned to the Aldens. "Wait here," he said. He went to the shed and came out with two small balloons on strings. He handed one to Soo Lee and one to Benny. "When I give the signal, let these balloons go," he directed.

Violet looked puzzled. These were ordinary party balloons. She couldn't imagine why they were needed.

Sky answered her unspoken question. "These balloons are filled with helium. Like hot air, it's lighter than the surrounding atmosphere. We use them to test the winds."

Matt said, "Now!" and Soo Lee and Benny released the balloons.

Everyone watched the balloons climb and drift. Finally satisfied that they had enough information to make successful flights, the balloonists hurried to their launch sites.

Sky and Matt were not going up today, so they didn't need the Aldens' help. "You can watch Don get ready," Sky suggested.

Don and his crew unpacked their balloon and carefully spread it over the ground. Then, they installed the propane tanks in the basket and tipped it on its side.

"Getting ready to fly is a lot of work," Benny observed.

"Yes, it is," Don said. "Especially with my crew, they're so slow," he complained.

"And it has to be done correctly," Henry said, "or they may have trouble."

Finally, all the equipment was in place and the cables and ropes attached. The crew chief tested everything. Then, he started a gasoline-powered fan. Two crew members lifted the edges of the balloon, opening it to let in the fan's airstream.

"Henry, you were certainly right," Violet

commented. "Pete Moran couldn't have launched Brad Golder's balloon alone."

"It might have taken more than two people," Jessie said.

Held down by crew members, the colorful balloon puffed up, swaying gently in the breeze. Don Fister ducked inside.

"Why is he going inside the balloon?" Soo Lee asked.

"He's checking for tears," Jessie answered.

"And he's making sure the opening in the top of the balloon is closed tightly," Henry said. "It's called the crown," he added.

"Why is there an opening in the top of the balloon?" Benny asked. "If it has to be closed anyway . . ."

"It's called a deflation port," Henry explained. "When the pilot wants to come down, he pulls a cord to open it."

Now Benny understood. He nodded. "And that lets air out."

Don Fister emerged from inside the balloon. "Now for some heat," he said. He turned a valve and lit the burner. With a loud *whoosh*, a yellow-blue flame shot through the balloon's mouth, heating the air inside.

Pete Moran, a volunteer crew member, turned off the fan. Others held tight to the balloon ropes. As Don directed a series of heat bursts into the balloon covering, the balloon struggled to be free.

"Ease off!" the crew chief shouted, and the rope handlers loosened their hold.

Then, Don gave the order to let go of the ropes. The balloon rose, swaying, to an upright position.

"It's going to take off!" Mary England cried.

The crew rushed forward. Mary joined them. They grabbed hold of the basket just as Don Fister hopped inside.

After one last check, Don released another blast of heat. "Hands off!" he instructed, and everyone stood back.

The balloon and basket rose slowly skyward.

"Wow!" Benny exclaimed. "Look at it go!"

Pete Moran started his station wagon. Another volunteer hopped into the passenger seat. They would follow Don's balloon to its landing site.

Everyone else was busy preparing their own balloons for flight. Before long, five more balloons took off, filling the sky with brilliant color.

"Quite a sight, isn't it?" Matt said.

"It sure is!" the Aldens agreed.

Five cars pulled out of the port.

"There go the chase crews," Benny observed.

Mary England came up beside them. "I ripped my stockings on that basket," she said.

"You shouldn't have grabbed the basket like that," Matt said. "That's the crew's job."

Mary ignored him. "I'm going home to change," she said. "I'll be back later."

"Take your time," Matt said, but Mary was already headed for her car.

One hour later, Brad Golder and his chase crew returned.

"I couldn't find Fister anywhere," Brad told them. "It was as if he just . . . disappeared."

One after another, the balloonists returned, each with the same story: Don Fister was nowhere to be found. The Hare and Hounds contest was canceled.

"That's strange," Sky said. "He's a good pilot, and we marked the maps with the best landing spots."

"He'll turn up," Matt assured her.

When Pete returned without Don, even Matt looked worried.

"Don wasn't following the course, and we just couldn't keep up with him," Pete said.

"Maybe we should all go looking for him," Benny suggested.

Sky shook her head. "If his own crew couldn't find him . . ." Her voice trailed off.

"Is there anything we *can* do?" Jessie asked.

Sky shrugged. "Pete can take the chase crew out for another search, and we can wait here to see if Don calls," she answered.

CHAPTER 8

Return of the Hare

During the long tense wait, Sky, Matt, and the Aldens sat near the shed and talked about ballooning.

Suddenly, Violet spotted something across the field. It moved steadily toward them, a cloud of dust swirling in its wake. "Is that a truck?" she asked.

Sky got to her feet. "Looks like it," she said.

Matt shielded his eyes with his hand. "It's a pickup. There's a basket in the back."

"I'll bet it's Don Fister," Benny said.

They hurried toward the oncoming truck and met it where it stopped. Don Fister jumped down from the passenger side. His round face was pinched with anger.

"What happened?" Matt asked.

"Are you all right?" Sky wanted to know.

He waved away their questions. "Help me get my gear," he said sternly.

Henry and Jessie scrambled into the back of the truck. They began moving equipment toward the tailgate. The others lifted it and set it on the ground. The driver turned the truck around.

"Thanks for everything!" Don called after him as he drove away. Then, he turned toward Sky and Matt. "You want to know what happened? I'll tell you what happened! I didn't have a map. That's what happened."

Sky was stunned. "But I gave everyone a map."

"And my compass — that was gone, too!"

"Did you have them when you launched?" Matt asked.

"Yes, I had the map and the compass," Don snapped. "I checked. My crew chief checked. They were in the basket where they belong."

"Could they have fallen out?" Benny asked.

"The basket was on its side when you were inflating the balloon," Henry reminded Don. "Maybe they fell out then."

Don stomped over to the basket. He reached in and pulled out several maps. "I have these. They didn't . . . fall out. Can you explain that?"

No one could.

Don answered his own question. "Nothing fell out! Someone stole my map and my compass — that's what happened."

"But who?" Sky said. "No one would do such a thing."

Don began to pace. "I was lucky to find that farmer's field. And lucky he was so helpful. I don't know how I would've gotten back here without him."

"You could have phoned. Someone

would've picked you up," Matt said.

A crowd had gathered. Everyone wanted to know what had happened. Don told and retold his story.

Henry said, "Let's go sit in the shade." He started toward the big oak. The other Aldens followed.

"Do you think Don's right?" Violet asked. "Someone took the map and compass?"

"Yes," Jessie answered. "Why would one map fall out of the basket and not the others?"

"Someone would have found them if they'd fallen on the ground," Soo Lee suggested.

"Right," Henry said. "Someone must have taken them."

"But who?" Benny asked.

"And when?" Violet said.

They fell silent, each trying to remember what had happened before the balloon went up.

"Pete was a crew member," Jessie said at last.

Henry nodded. "He could have removed

the map and compass at any time."

"Don and his crew chief checked everything," Soo Lee reminded them.

Benny nodded. "More than once," he said.

"Whoever took those things must have done it at the very last minute," Violet concluded.

"Pete held the basket down," Jessie remembered.

"Other crew members did that, too," Henry said.

"Mary England helped," Soo Lee reminded them.

"Whoever took Don's things probably launched Brad Golder's balloon, too," Henry suggested.

"We've got another mystery to solve," Benny concluded.

The sun was a blazing ball low in the western sky.

"It must be near dinnertime," Benny said. "Let's go see if Sky and Matt are ready to go back to the inn."

The Aldens trooped over to the shed. Sky

and Matt were talking to Mary.

"Mary changed more than her stockings," Soo Lee observed.

Mary was wearing a white dress patterned with small lavender flowers.

"That's a pretty dress," Violet said. She liked anything colored with shades of purple.

When she saw the Aldens, Sky excused herself and joined them.

"Is it time to go back to the inn?" Jessie asked.

"Barbara will serve dinner soon," Sky answered. "But Matt and I are staying here. We have to go over tomorrow's schedule."

"You mean you'll go without dinner?" Benny asked. He couldn't imagine anyone skipping a meal.

"Matt'll drive into town and pick up something," Sky told him.

"We can get a ride back to the inn with Pete," Henry suggested.

Coming up beside them, Mary said, "Pete went on ahead. I'm dining at the inn; I'll be happy to take you."

"Thank you," the Aldens said.

They followed Mary to her car.

Inside, Benny said, "It's awful hot in here. How do you open the windows?"

"I never open the windows," Mary responded. "They let in too much dust and dirt." She pushed a button. "I always use the air-conditioning."

Barbara had vegetables and dip awaiting them in the parlor.

Benny dug right in. "This is good," he said.

"Don't eat too much," Barbara told him. "I wouldn't want you to spoil your appetite for dinner."

Henry chuckled. "No chance of that, is there, Benny?"

"I can always eat," Benny assured Barbara.

Pete came in from the kitchen. He nodded at Mary. "Hello, Mary," he said. "I didn't know you were coming to dinner."

"There are many things you don't know,"

Mary replied. Her tone was sharp.

Barbara glanced at the clock on the mantle. "I wonder what's keeping Hollis," she said.

Pete smiled at the Aldens. "How'd you like your first day of ballooning?"

"It was exciting," Henry answered.

"First there was a runaway balloon," Soo Lee said.

"And then Don Fister's balloon disappeared," Violet added.

And the Hare and Hounds game was ruined because Don Fister was the hare," Benny said.

Pete grinned. "That was one rabbit we couldn't pull out of the hat," he joked.

The Aldens laughed. Barbara and Mary did not.

A tense silence followed.

After a while, Jessie said, "The lunch Pete brought to the port was very good. Did you make it, Barbara?"

Barbara looked pleased. "Yes, I did make it."

"It was delicious," Benny put in. "I had some of everything."

"We like picnics," Soo Lee added.

Henry told them all about living in the boxcar and the picnics they had enjoyed there. "Today reminded us of those times," he concluded.

"All that was missing was our blue tablecloth and my pink cup," Benny said.

Jessie explained how they had come to own those things.

Barbara seemed very interested. "Blue tablecloth and pink cup," she murmured as though she were storing information in her memory.

Hollis McKnight arrived, and they all went into the dining room.

Looking at the table, Benny's eyes grew large. "Oh, boy," he said. "Roasted chicken! My favorite!"

Jessie said, "Oh, Benny, everything's your favorite."

This time, even Barbara and Mary laughed.

During dinner, Mary and Hollis did most of the talking. They told stories about

Lloyd's Landing — its early history and development.

"It sounds as if Lloyd's Landing hasn't changed much over the years," Henry commented.

"Exactly," Mary responded. "Our grandparents — Barbara's and mine — wanted a quiet, peaceful place. We've all tried to honor their wishes."

"Sometimes, things can be too peaceful," Hollis said.

Mary shot him a withering glance. Then, she said, "I'm sorry to eat and run, but I must go." She thanked Barbara for the dinner and headed for the door.

"Will we see you tomorrow at the rally?" Pete asked.

The Aldens were sure she heard him; yet, she didn't respond.

After a strawberry shortcake dessert, Hollis McKnight looked at his watch. "I have to get back to the paper," he said. "Put it to bed."

Benny imagined him tucking a newspaper

into a small bed. He giggled. "That's funny," he said. "A newspaper going to bed."

Hollis laughed heartily. "It is a strange expression," he admitted. "It means going to press."

After he had gone, Barbara began clearing the table. Violet and Soo Lee gathered the silverware. When they took it into the kitchen, Barbara was on the phone.

Her face reddened and she put down the receiver. "Line's busy," she said.

"May we help you with the dishes?" Violet asked.

"No, thank you, dear," Barbara answered.

Pete suggested they go outside to sit on the porch. "It's nice this time of night."

Henry and Benny sat on a wooden swing. Violet, Jessie, and Soo Lee settled into rocking chairs. Pete sat on the top step. No one spoke. Fireflies flickered on the lawn, and the stars twinkled in the night sky.

After a while, Benny yawned. "I'm really tired," he said.

"You'd better get a good night's sleep,"

Pete said. "We're up before dawn tomorrow."

"Just a few more minutes," Soo Lee pleaded.

Benny yawned again. "I'll meet you upstairs," he said. "I'm going to get a glass of milk and then go to bed."

Inside, he heard Barbara talking to someone. He crept into the kitchen so as not to disturb her. She was on the phone, her back to him.

She said, "Drop it," sternly.

Benny felt uncomfortable. The telephone conversation was private; Barbara would not be happy that he had overheard.

Suddenly, Barbara realized she was not alone. She put down the receiver and turned to Benny. Smiling uneasily, she asked, "What can I do for you, Benny?"

"Oh, nothing," Benny said, and he ran up the stairs.

CHAPTER 9

The Missing Ad

Benny was dreaming he was floating above Lloyd's Landing in a balloon. Suddenly, everything began to shake.

"Benny, wake up," Henry urged him.

Benny rolled over. "I have to land first," he mumbled.

"It's time to go out to the port," Henry said.

Benny opened his eyes and stretched. "I thought I was already there," he said. While he dressed, he told Henry about his dream.

"I dreamed about ballooning, too," Henry said.

The girls came in.

"Aren't you ready yet?" Jessie teased.

"Soon as I find my other shoe," Benny said. He looked under the bed. There it was.

Violet said, "Take your time. Barbara told us she would let us know when breakfast is ready."

"You must've stayed downstairs late last night," Benny said. "I tried to stay awake because I had something to tell you, but I couldn't keep my eyes open."

Soo Lee sat down on the edge of the bed. "Tell us now."

"Well, I went into the kitchen for a glass of milk before bed," Benny began. "And I found Barbara talking on the phone — she was arguing with somebody!"

"About what?" Henry asked.

Benny shook his head. "I don't know. All I heard her say was 'drop it.' And she was angry."

"Barbara was on the phone earlier," Violet remembered.

Soo Lee nodded. "And she hung up when she saw us."

"That's what she did when she saw me," Benny told them.

"Do you suppose the phone calls had anything to do with what happened out at the port?" Jessie asked.

"Sounds like it," Henry said.

"Barbara and Pete are so nice," Violet said. "It's hard to believe that they have anything to do with this."

"Why would they want to ruin the balloon business?" Soo Lee asked. "It would be good for the inn."

"But who else could have launched Brad's balloon and taken Don's map and compass?" Henry said.

They all thought about that for a while.

Finally, Violet suggested, "Don Fister could have done it. He was at the port early yesterday morning. Maybe his crew chief helped him launch the balloon."

"And he could have just pretended his map was gone," Soo Lee said.

"That's possible," Jessie admitted. "He doesn't seem to want the business to succeed."

"He has his own balloon business," Henry reminded them. "He might think that's a reason to ruin Sky and Matt's."

Barbara knocked at the door. "Breakfast," she announced.

Benny was the first one out the door.

"Where are Matt and Sky?" Jessie asked as they entered the dining room.

"Oh, they left very early," said Barbara. "They wanted to get there before the other balloonists."

They ate a hearty breakfast of sausage, pancakes, and scrambled eggs.

"I am so full," Benny said. "I don't think I'll ever be able to eat again."

Barbara laughed. "Oh, I'm quite sure you'll be hungry by noon. Especially when you see what I've prepared for you." She went into the kitchen and came back with a basket. "In here is your own special picnic lunch." She handed the basket to Henry. "Now run along. Pete's waiting for you outside."

The Aldens thanked Barbara for the picnic basket and met Pete outside.

Pete drove them out to the balloon port. By the time they arrived, the sun had begun to paint the eastern sky with faint streaks of pinkish light.

When they arrived, small groups of balloonists were scattered across the big field, already busy with their equipment.

Sky and Matt were huddled over the morning newspaper. They were obviously upset.

"What's wrong?" Pete asked them.

Sky thrust the paper at him. "Our ad! It's not in the paper!"

Pete did not take the paper from her outstretched hand. "It's not?!" he exclaimed, but he didn't really sound surprised.

A short distance away, Mary England slammed her car trunk. For a moment,

the sound distracted them all. Then Sky said, "Wait till I get hold of that Hollis McKnight!"

Smiling, Mary joined the group. Even in slacks and blouse, she looked dressed up. "Good morning," she greeted them. "Looks as though you'll have a *perfect* day for your rally."

"If anyone comes," Matt said, and told her about the missing ad.

Mary waved that away. "By the looks of things, you don't need more advertising. You'll have a large audience."

She was right. Spectators had gathered along the edges of the field and were continuing to arrive.

That didn't ease Sky. "I paid for that ad," she said. "He had no right to withdraw it."

Just then, Hollis McKnight pulled in and got out of his car.

Waving the paper, Sky marched toward him. "Did you do this?!" she demanded.

Hollis tilted his head to look through the

bottom half of his glasses. "Did I do *what*?" he asked.

"Why didn't you run our ad?" Matt demanded.

Hollis looked confused. "Because you canceled it," he said.

CHAPTER 10

Grounded!

Sky's jaw dropped. "We never canceled the ad," she told Hollis.

"Well, someone did," Hollis said.

"When?" Matt asked.

"Last night. My assistant took the phone message."

The Aldens exchanged glances. Each of them was remembering what Benny had overheard: "Drop it," Barbara had said. Had she phoned the newspaper to cancel the ad?

"It was so late, I had nothing to fill the space," Hollis was saying. "The only thing I could do was enlarge The Landing's Inn ad."

Don Fister rushed up to them. "Are we going to fly today or not?" he asked.

"Yes, yes," Sky answered. "Is everyone ready?"

"We're all waiting for you," he said.

She handed him another map. "Do you have a compass?" she asked.

He nodded. "I borrowed one."

The morning's event was a time–distance race. Each pilot and crew would begin to inflate their balloons on cue. They would then lift off, go as far as possible, and land within an hour's time. Whoever went the farthest would win.

Sky and Matt were going to participate in this event. Matt took Sky's arm. "Let's get ready," he said, and led her and the Aldens to their spot on the field. "I'm crew chief," Matt told the Aldens. "Just follow my orders."

With the Aldens' help, Sky and Matt spread out their red-white-and-blue nylon covering. Other members of the crew grabbed propane tanks and secured them inside the basket. They tipped the basket on its side and placed the burner and instruments. Next, they sorted out the cables and ropes and attached them to the proper places.

Matt started the fan. He told everyone to grab hold of the lines to steady the balloon. They promptly obeyed.

"Benny! Step to one side! You're in the way of the fan!" Sky instructed.

The fan had whipped Benny's hair into a mass of untidy curls.

"It looks like you combed your hair with an eggbeater," Henry teased.

Busy with his assigned job, Benny ignored him.

Sky checked the inside of the balloon. "It looks okay," she said. "Now, let's give it some heat." She reached for the blast valve. Her hand stopped in midair. "Turn off the fan," she shouted.

Matt did so. "What's wrong?" he asked.

"One of the propane tanks is missing," Sky told him.

Matt looked inside the basket. "They were all out here earlier. I lined up all the equipment myself."

Sky threw up her hands. "We can't go up."

Benny glanced at the tanks. They were big. They must hold lots of propane gas. "Can't you go up with what you have?"

Sky shook her head. "It'd be taking a chance," she explained. "And a good pilot doesn't take chances."

"Can't you get another tank?" Violet asked.

Matt shook his head. "No time," he said.

Pete had already announced the start of the race over the loudspeaker and some of the balloons had left the ground.

Mary, Hollis, and Pete came over to see what was going on.

Henry told them what had happened.

"Oh, my, more trouble," Mary commented.

She sounded as though she had expected it.

"Well, I'm certainly not going to sit here feeling sorry for myself," Sky said. She turned to Pete. "Does everyone have a chase crew?"

"I'm it for Don," he answered. "He did so much complaining most of his crew quit."

"All right," Sky said. "We'll go with you."

"Take our van," Matt suggested. "There's more room."

"Let's move," Pete urged. "Don's already airborne!"

Sky, Matt, Pete, and the Aldens dashed for the van. Matt climbed in the driver's side.

Sky handed Benny and Jessie maps. "You be the navigators," she said. "The rest of us will keep Don in sight."

That was easier said than done. Don's yellow, orange, and green balloon disappeared now and then — behind the tree line, over a ridge. No one spoke as the van moved up one country road and down another. Periodically, the walkie-talkie Pete held squawked.

Don's voice would come through, broken by static.

Benny followed their course on the map. "This is hard," he said.

Jessie compared her readings with his. "What's hard is that we're down here and he's up there."

"But it's exciting," Soo Lee commented.

Everyone agreed with that.

"The hour's almost up," Violet said, looking at her watch.

"I wonder whose balloon went the farthest?" Benny asked.

Next Don's voice came over the walkie-talkie and said that he'd found a landing spot and would soon come down.

Jessie and Benny located the spot on the map and directed Matt toward it. Near the landing site, Matt eased the van to the side of the road and stopped.

"Everybody out," Sky directed.

They piled out of the van and ran up an embankment and across an open field. Above them, Don was slowly coming down. He threw out a tow rope. Matt grabbed it. As the basket touched down, the others grabbed the ropes on the side. The basket bounced and toppled.

Don crawled out, smiling. "You're looking at a winner!" he said confidently.

He didn't seem a bit surprised to see Sky and Matt. How could he possibly know that they had not gone up in their own balloon?

They packed up the balloon and headed back to the field to see how the other balloonists had done.

Sure enough: Don was the winner. He had flown several miles beyond Brad Golder, who came in second.

The Aldens overheard Brad complain to Sky. "Don should be disqualified from the next event," he said. "He wins everything."

Sky shrugged. "He is an excellent balloonist."

Pete brought the picnic basket to the Aldens. "I thought you might be hungry after that chase," he told them.

"Are we ever!" Benny said.

"Are you going to eat with us?" Jessie asked.

Pete shook his head. "I'm going to go back to the inn — see if Barbara needs help with anything. I'll see you later."

The children headed for the oak tree.

"I wonder if Don would have won if Sky and Matt had been in the race," Henry commented.

"And why wasn't he surprised to see Matt and Sky when they were supposed to be in the race?" Violet asked.

"Maybe he was so excited about winning he didn't notice," Soo Lee suggested.

"Do you think Don took the propane tank?" Jessie asked him.

Henry shrugged. "I don't know."

"He had more reason than Pete or Barbara," Violet said.

"And he could have done the other things," Soo Lee added.

"But what about Sky's ad?" Benny asked. "Barbara was the one who called Mr. McKnight."

"We don't know that for sure, Benny," Jessie said. "She could have been phoning . . . anybody."

"I think Pete did it," Benny said. "Pete and Barbara. Or maybe Barbara and . . . Mary."

Henry let out a surprised breath. "Barbara and Mary? They don't even like each other."

Benny shrugged. "Maybe they're just pretending."

Violet didn't think so. "They don't like each other — that's for sure."

Jessie opened the picnic basket. "Look at this!" She pulled out a small blue tablecloth.

"And look here!" Benny extracted a cup. "It isn't cracked like mine, but it's pink!"

Soo Lee said, "How nice of Barbara."

"She is really thoughtful," Violet said.

"Too thoughtful to be mixed up in all this," Henry decided.

Benny nodded. "I guess you're right," he said.

CHAPTER 11

The Confession

Pete arrived and crossed the field to the oak tree. "I left the back of the station wagon open," he told the Aldens. "Just put the picnic basket inside when you're finished."

Squinting toward the station wagon, Henry asked, "Did Barbara come back with you?"

"Yes," Pete answered. "She wanted to see for herself what this ballooning is all about."

They finished lunch and headed across the field.

"Where'd Barbara go?" Jessie wondered aloud. "I'd like to thank her."

"I see her!" Benny said. "She's over by the shed with everyone else."

"Jessie, why don't you and Henry go talk to her," Violet suggested. "We'll take the things to the wagon."

"We'll meet you by the shed," Henry said as he and Jessie started toward it.

Pete's station wagon was parked between Sky's van and Mary's car. As they hoisted the picnic basket into it, Soo Lee noticed something.

"What are you looking at?" Benny asked her.

Soo Lee moved closer to Mary's car. "Something is sticking out of Mary's car trunk," she said.

Benny came up beside her. "Let me see what it is."

Violet said, "It looks like . . ."

". . . a bandanna!" all three exclaimed.

"A blue-and-white bandanna," Soo Lee said.

Benny tugged at it. It slipped out easily.

"Look in the corner," Violet told him.

Benny held the scarf so that they could all see the letters *B. G.* inked there. "Brad Golder's other bandanna!"

"We'd better get Jessie and Henry," Violet said.

"I'll find them," Soo Lee volunteered and ran off.

Benny shook his head in disbelief. "Do you think Mary England is doing all this?" he asked.

Violet was thinking the same thing.

Henry was the first to reach them. "What's up?" he asked.

At his heels, Jessie said, "Soo Lee said you found an important clue."

Benny held up the bandanna. "It's important all right."

"Where did you find that?" Henry asked.

"Sticking out of Mary's car," Violet answered.

"Mary England?" Jessie said.

"It's hard to believe one person could have done all this," Henry said.

"Maybe Mary found the bandanna," Soo Lee suggested.

"Pete said he found the red one," Benny reminded them.

"And Mary told us she saw Pete on Mill Road," Violet reminded them. "She could have found this bandanna where Pete found the other one."

"If she did, why didn't she mention it?" Jessie wanted to know.

No one could answer that. Mary had been there when Brad discovered the red bandanna in Pete's pocket. If she had found one, too, she would have spoken up.

"Maybe she did the other things," Soo Lee said, "but she couldn't have launched the balloon alone."

They all agreed that seemed unlikely.

"Maybe the whole town is in on this," Benny said.

That was certainly a possibility. No one

seemed to welcome the balloonists and their business.

They fell silent, thinking.

Suddenly, Jessie remembered something. "Mary launched Brad's balloon all right," she said with certainty.

"What makes you so sure?" Henry asked her.

"Her hair," Jessie answered.

For several seconds, no one understood what she meant.

Then, Benny spoke up. "I've got it!" he said. "That day her hair was all messed up!"

"And there was no wind," Soo Lee remembered.

"And," Violet added, "she never opens her car windows."

"The fan messed up her hair just like it messed up mine!" Benny concluded.

"I think you're right," Jessie said.

"But who helped her?" Violet asked.

No one responded.

"What about Sky's ad?" Benny asked. "Barbara canceled that."

"We don't know who Barbara was talking to," Jessie said. "We already decided that."

"Mary did have the chance to steal Don's map and compass," Soo Lee said.

"That's right," Benny said. "She helped his crew hold the basket down."

"She probably took Sky's gas tank, too," Soo Lee decided.

Henry said, "I think it's time we talk to Mary."

The Aldens walked toward the shed. Henry held the blue-and-white bandanna. It fluttered in the breeze like a flag.

Brad Golder was the first to notice it. "My bandanna!" he said as the children approached. "Where did you find it?"

"Right in Mary England's trunk," Benny blurted.

Mary's mouth dropped open and her eyes grew big. "My trunk?!" she sputtered. "What — ? Why — ? How — ?

Brad Golder turned on her. "So it was you!"

Sky's bright face darkened. "I should have known," she said.

Mary backed away. "I don't know what you're talking about. I had nothing to do with your balloon, Brad. I had nothing to do with any of this."

Everyone was staring at her.

She reddened. "I — I . . . found the scarf," she continued. "I found it out on Mill Road where Pete found the other one." She shot Hollis McKnight a pleading glance. "Isn't that so, Hollis? You remember. Out on Mill Road? Near the spring?"

"It's no use, Mary," Hollis responded. "This whole thing has been wrong from the start. We have to tell the truth." He looked at Matt and Sky. "We — I thought it was best for the community. I was afraid this ballooning business would change Lloyd's Landing forever. I didn't want that. I love this town. So I agreed to help Mary stop it."

Brad nodded. "So you two launched my balloon."

"That's how Mary's hair got messed up," Benny put in.

"We didn't know it was your balloon," Hollis assured Brad. "It was the easiest one to launch. Smaller than some of the others, and everything was set out and ready."

"How did the red bandanna end up out by the spring?" Pete asked.

"Launching a balloon is hard work — especially for two inexperienced people," Hollis explained. "Afterward, we stopped at the spring for a drink. The bandannas were stuffed in my pocket. One must have fallen out."

"And I found it," Pete said.

"Did you have anything to do with Don's missing map and compass?" Henry asked.

Hollis shook his head. "No, no. Nothing. I realized that I had been wrong. I wanted nothing more to do with any of it."

"What made you change your mind?" Jessie asked Hollis.

"The letters," Hollis answered. "Hundreds of letters in answer to my editorial. It seemed there were just a few townspeople who objected to the balloon business. Everyone else was in favor of it."

The Aldens remembered the conversation between Hollis and Mary here at the port. He had taken a stack of letters out of a big brown envelope and waved them in her face.

"I tried to tell Mary to stop interfering, but she wouldn't listen," Hollis went on.

Had Mary done the other things by herself? Henry wondered. Or was someone else involved?

"But what about Sky's ad?" Benny wanted to know. "I heard Barbara on the phone. She said, 'Drop it.' "

Barbara stepped forward. "I didn't cancel that ad. I was phoning Mary to tell her to stop this nonsense. I thought she was right at first: The ballooning business would destroy Lloyd's Landing. But it was tearing us apart. Pete and Mary were friends and now . . ."

Pete spoke up. "I knew the business would be good for the inn — for the whole town!

How could I go along with a plan to ruin it?"

"After Mary left the inn last night, I called her. The line was busy," Barbara continued.

"Later, I phoned again. We got into an argument. I said some dreadful things. Finally, I just told her to drop the whole thing."

Mary had listened quietly. Now, with her arms crossed over her chest, she rocked gently back and forth. "I am so sorry," she said. "I didn't mean to hurt anyone. I just didn't want Lloyd's Landing to change. When I was young, I thought this town was dull and boring. I left it, but I soon learned that it's a special place."

"That's why we chose it," Sky told her.

"Ballooning would make it even more special," Violet said softly.

"I didn't think so," Mary said. "I thought it would ruin everything."

"You're the one who tried to ruin everything," Matt said.

"I hoped you and Sky would change your minds. Go somewhere else. That's why I called up Hollis's assistant, and canceled the ad. I thought if no one came to the rally, you'd reconsider."

"But it didn't work," Benny said.

Mary sighed. "Nothing worked. I thought Don would cause real trouble when his map and compass were missing, but . . ." Her voice trailed off.

Sky huffed. "Don doesn't need your help to cause trouble," she said.

Pete understood what Mary meant. "But all Don did was complain," he said.

Henry chuckled. "He always does that."

Mary nodded. "Yes, so no one took him seriously."

"Did you take our propane tank?" Matt asked.

Mary nodded. "I was sure someone would see me lugging that heavy thing. But everyone was busy. No one noticed."

In his mind, Benny heard Mary's car trunk slam shut as it had early this morning. "It's in your trunk," he murmured.

"I was sure you wouldn't go up without

it," Mary said to Sky. "I thought if something happened to keep you from flying, you might just . . . give up."

"Wrong again," Matt commented.

"Ballooning will be good for the businesses in town," Jessie said.

"For The Landing's Inn and all the inns and hotels," Henry added.

"And the restaurants," Benny put in.

"For the whole town," Soo Lee said.

"And it doesn't harm the environment," Violet said.

Mary nodded. "I'm beginning to see that," she said. "Still, the idea of change . . ."

"We don't want to change Lloyd's Landing," Sky assured her. "We just want to be a part of it." She put her arm around Mary's shoulders. "I'll tell you what: We'll take you for a ride. You can see for yourself how wonderful ballooning is."

Mary's face opened with surprise. "You'd do that? After all the trouble I've caused?"

Sky laughed. "Believe me, one ride, and you'll be our biggest supporter."

CHAPTER 12

Up, Up, and Away

Sky was right. Mary was a changed person when she returned from her flight. "I'll never again condemn something I know nothing about," she said. Then, she offered to take posters announcing the rally to every store in town. "I'll even put them up out near the highway to attract more business."

Matt said, "Thank you, but we don't need more publicity."

"We'll keep you busy, though," Sky said.

"It looks as if this will be a very busy, very successful rally."

She was right about that, too.

The remaining events that day went smoothly. The weather was perfect: clear skies, light breezes. The competitors helped one another. Even Don Fister softened. The Aldens overheard him giving tips to other balloonists.

"Your business will do fine," Don told Sky and Matt. "And it'll be good for my business."

They were all surprised at his change of heart.

Benny asked, "Why will it be good for your business?"

"The more people we can interest in the sport, the better it is for everybody," he explained. He sounded as if he had always believed that.

As busy as the Aldens were with launching and chasing, they found a few quiet moments. They sat under the oak tree. Sometimes, they talked about the mystery they had solved. Sometimes, they would be silent, each lost in his or her own thoughts. Sometimes, Violet would sketch. Her drawings were full of colorful balloons and bright skies.

"I wonder what's it's like," Soo Lee said.

They all knew what she meant. Each was trying to imagine what it would be like to float over the countryside.

"We'll soon find out," Henry responded enthusiastically.

"Tomorrow at sunset," Jessie added.

That night, Barbara and Pete had a barbecue. All the balloonists and their crews attended it. Mary England and Hollis McKnight were there, too.

"I'd like to make up for the missing ad," Hollis told Sky. "I thought I'd run a full-page story about ballooning. Perhaps you and Matt could write it."

Sky shook her head. "Writing an ad is one thing," she said, "but I couldn't write an entire article."

"Count me out, too," Matt said.

"Henry's a good writer," Benny offered. "Maybe he could do it."

"Oh, Benny, please, I couldn't write anything," Henry said, but he had been thinking the same thing.

Hollis tilted his head and looked at Henry through the bottom half of his glasses. "How about it, son?" he said. "Would you like to give it a try?"

Henry gulped. "Really?" he said.

Hollis smiled. "Really."

"Yes, sir, I'd like that," Henry decided. "Jessie could help. She knows a lot about ballooning." He looked at Jessie. There was a question in his eyes.

Jessie's smile was an enthusiastic yes.

"Good," Hollis said. "Now, you have to understand, I don't print every article sent to me."

"Oh, you'll print this one," Benny said. "It'll be very good."

"And you could use Violet's drawings," Soo Lee said.

Violet blushed. "Oh, Soo Lee, I don't know."

Hollis was delighted. "Story *and* illustrations! Perfect!"

"Now that that's settled," Benny said, "let's eat!"

On their way to the table, Matt said, "You certainly are a talented family."

Sky nodded agreement. "That's for sure," she said. "Writers, artists — "

"Don't forget detectives," Benny put in with a grin on his face.

Sky nodded again. "And very good ones at that. We never would have solved this mystery without you."

The evening ended early. Everyone wanted to be rested for the last day's events.

The Aldens gathered in the girls' bedroom where they sat up talking for a short time.

"Strange how things work out," Henry commented.

"What do you mean, Henry?" Violet asked.

"Well, take Mary. She's really interested in ballooning now. I'll bet she keeps volunteering to help."

Jessie understood what he meant. "And if she hadn't been so against the business to begin with, she might not have come out to the port at all."

"It's lucky Mary didn't hurt anybody," Benny reminded them.

"She was careful not to do anything dangerous," Henry said.

"Still," Soo Lee put in, "she had no right to do the things she did."

They all agreed with that.

Henry stretched and yawned. "We'd better get to bed," he said and crossed into the other room.

Benny followed. "I'll be up all night," he said. "I'm so excited about tomorrow." But he fell asleep the minute he laid his head on the pillow.

* * *

Next morning, when Sky and Matt drove the Aldens to the port, it was still dark. Yet, everyone was busy readying for flight. Several balloonists ascended as the day's first light appeared in the sky.

Still sleepy, Soo Lee asked, "Why do the balloonists like to fly so early?"

"Dawn and sunset are the best times," Sky answered.

"The sun has an effect on the wind," Matt explained. "During the middle of the day, the breezes are usually too strong."

Violet got out her sketchbook. "It's hard to tell which is prettier," she said. "The sunrise or the balloons."

Because they were excited about their own flight, the Aldens thought the day would seem long, but they were wrong. When Sky said, "Well, are you ready for your great adventure?" they were surprised the time had come.

Mary, Pete, Brad, and Don volunteered to be their crew. Matt was the crew chief.

Once the balloon was inflated and straining to be free, they took hold of the basket to steady it. The Aldens climbed over the padded sides into the basket.

"Make yourself comfortable," Sky told them.

That was difficult to do in such a small space. But no one complained.

Sky opened the blast valve. *Whooosssbhh!* The yellow-blue flame roared into the bulging bag.

There was a tug on the basket.

"Is everybody clear?" Sky called.

Matt raised his arms toward the spectators. "Move back," he directed them. Then he said, "All clear" to Sky.

"Hands off!" Sky shouted.

The crew stepped away.

One more blast of heat and then everything went silent. In a few seconds, the world began to fall away. The people seemed to grow smaller.

"Are they moving or are we?" Benny wanted to know.

Sky laughed. "We're moving all right. Look around you."

Sure enough, they were already above the treetops.

Sky skillfully maneuvered the balloon higher and higher. Below them, everything was in its place, neat and orderly.

"It's like a patchwork quilt," Jessie said.

Benny giggled. "Look!" he said.

Below them, a dog ran through a field, barking at them. All along their route, people came out of their houses or stopped their work in the fields to wave. Miniature cars moved along the roads. Some of them pulled to the side of the road to watch them pass. To the west, the sun had slipped into the slot between earth and sky like a bright copper coin into a piggy bank. It left behind a brilliant display of color.

Violet gasped. "I've never seen anything more beautiful."

Soo Lee spotted the chase crew. "There's the van," she said.

Then, for a long time, no one said anything. Now and then, the *whoosh* of the burner sounded. Otherwise, everything was silent.

Suddenly, Henry pointed to a station wagon making its way toward Lloyd's Landing. "That looks like Grandfather's car."

"It is! It is!" Benny exclaimed. "Wait till he hears about everything!"

Jessie laughed. "You certainly got your wish, Benny," she said. "No one could hope for a better adventure."

GERTRUDE CHANDLER WARNER discovered when she was teaching that many readers who like an exciting story could find no books that were both easy and fun to read. She decided to try to meet this need, and her first book, *The Boxcar Children*, quickly proved she had succeeded.

Miss Warner drew on her own experiences to write the mystery. As a child she spent hours watching trains go by on the tracks opposite her family home. She often dreamed about what it would be like to set up housekeeping in a caboose or freight car — the situation the Alden children find themselves in.

When Miss Warner received requests for more adventures involving Henry, Jessie, Violet, and Benny Alden, she began additional stories. In each, she chose a special setting and introduced unusual or eccentric characters who liked the unpredictable.

While the mystery element is central to each of Miss Warner's books, she never thought of them as strictly juvenile mysteries. She liked to stress the Aldens' independence and resourcefulness and their solid New England devotion to using up and making do. The Aldens go about most of their adventures with as little adult supervision as possible — something else that delights young readers.

Miss Warner lived in Putnam, Connecticut, until her death in 1979. During her lifetime, she received hundreds of letters from girls and boys telling her how much they liked her books.